This book is to be returned on or before
the last date stamped below

For Jess, who is Ruth and Sue's,
for Benjamin, who is Rowan's,
and for Gianino, who is mine.

First published 1992
by Walker Books Ltd, 87 Vauxhall Walk
London SE11 5HJ

This edition published 1994

2 4 6 8 10 9 7 5 3

Printed in Hong Kong

British Library Cataloguing in Publication Data
A catalogue record for this book is
available from the British Library.

ISBN 0-7445-3612-X

My Little B~r~other

Debi Gliori

WALKER BOOKS
AND SUBSIDIARIES
LONDON • BOSTON • SYDNEY

My little brother is a pest.

He wakes me
up at dawn
with his
leaky teddy,

copies
everything
I do,

follows me
round like a
shadow,

and won't let me go to sleep at night.

Sometimes I wish my little brother would just disappear.

I tried
magicking
him away,

but he ate
my book
of spells.

I tried
sending him
to the moon,

but he got
the rocket
all wet.

I plastered
him with
vanishing
cream,

but
that
didn't
work.

I tried
feeding him
to a wild
beast,

but she
only yawned,
and got on with
finding a place to
have her kittens.

One night something woke me up.

It was dark. The wind was
making a whoo-whooing noise.
I looked to see if my little brother
was awake…

but his bed was empty.

I got up to go and look for him.

Maybe he was in the kitchen,
the little pest?

The
kitchen
was quiet.
He wasn't
there.

Maybe he was watching
television, the little menace?
I looked in the sitting room.

The sitting room was empty.
He wasn't there either.

I began to feel a bit worried.

Maybe the
vanishing
cream had
vanished him!

Maybe the
magic spell
had worked!

I was really worried.
I looked up the chimney…

Maybe the rocket had really taken
him to the moon! I remembered
how nice he was, when he wasn't

being a pest. I remembered how
small he was, my little brother.
I had a horrible thought...

Maybe wild animals had really
eaten him!

I nearly burst into tears.

And then I
heard a noise.
A strange sort of
noise, a sort of

prrprrrrrrrraOWprrrr

sort of noise.
The sound
came from
the linen
cupboard.
I peered
round the
door, and I saw …

our cat and five kittens!
And curled round them all
was my little brother.

Not vanished, not magicked, not
gone to the moon and not eaten
by wild animals. Just fast asleep.

And even though he is a pest,
I don't ever want my little
brother to disappear again!

MORE WALKER PAPERBACKS
For You to Enjoy

Also by Debi Gliori

NEW BIG SISTER

One moment Mum's off her food and the next she's eating marmalade and cold spaghetti sandwiches! What's going on? Mum's having a baby, of course. But the biggest surprise is yet to come! Ideal for preparing children for a new arrival.

0-7445-3610-3   £3.99

NEW BIG HOUSE

The hall is full of baby walkers, the kitchen is bursting with laundry and the living room is a Lego minefield… What the family in this lively book needs is a new big house. But finding one proves to be a big headache!

0-7445-3609-X   £3.99

WHEN I'M BIG

A small child ponders the advantages of being big.

"Interprets every child's fears and ambitions… Debi Gliori's illustrations are full of humorous detail which will find a wide audience among three and four-year-olds." *Valerie Bierman, The Scotsman*

0-7445-3125-X   £3.99